Edward Built A Rocketship
Text Copyright | Michael Rack
Illustration Copyright | Graham Ross
The rights of Michael Rack and Graham Ross to be
named as the author and illustrator of this work have
been asserted by them in accordance with the Copyright,
Designs and Patents Act, 1988

Published in 2016 by Hutton Grove
An imprint of Bravo Ltd.
Sales and Enquiries
Kuperard Publishers & Distributors
59 Hutton Grove, London, N12 8DS
United Kingdom
Tel: +44 (0)208 446 2440
Fax: +44 (0)208 446 2441
sales@kuperard.co.uk
www.kuperard.co.uk

Published by arrangement with Albury Books
Albury Court, Albury, Oxfordshire, OX9 2LP

ISBN 978-1-910925-13-3 (hardback)
ISBN 978-1-910925-12-6 (paperback)

A CIP catalogue record for this book is available from the
British Library
10 9 8 7 6 5 4 3
Printed in China

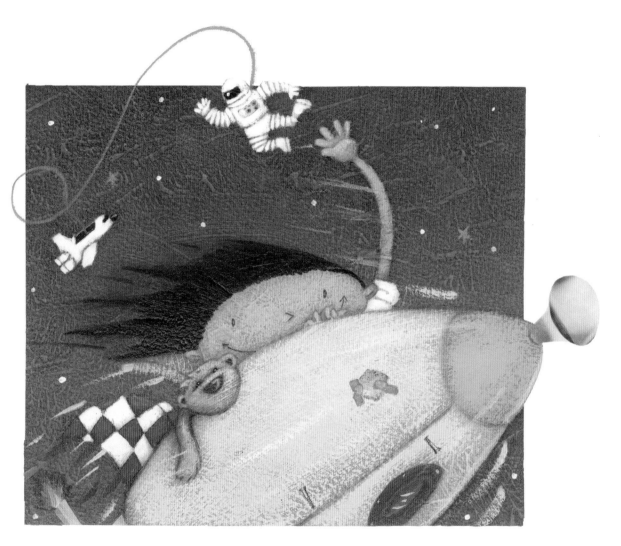

EDWARD BUILT A ROCKETSHIP

Michael Rack • *illustrated by Graham Ross*

"I'll do a dance on Venus,
And have a snack on Mars.

Edward looked into the sky
And said "I think I might
Shoot across the galaxy
At ten o'clock tonight.

I'll read a book on Saturn
By the light of all the stars."

The more he looked, the more he thought, about his master plan,
"I need to get myself up there as quickly as I can!"

He put things here,

        he put things there,

So Edward built a rocket ship,
Designed to fly so far.
He built it from some odds and ends
And parts from Daddy's car.

And added loads of stuff.

3

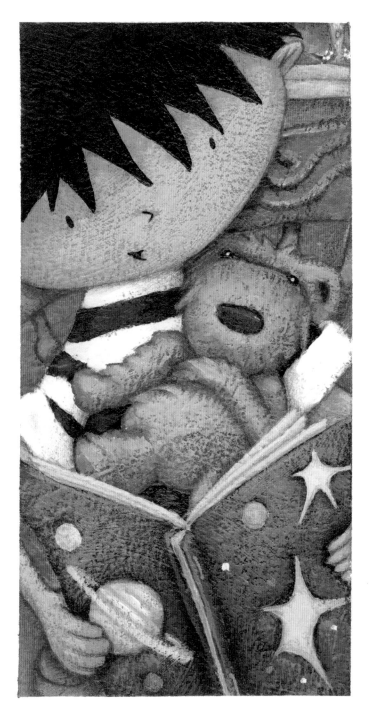

He even packed his teddy bear,
    In case it got too rough.

His mother kissed him on the nose
And handed him a snack.
    "Say hello to Mercury,
    But don't be too late back!"

4

He climbed into his rocket ship
And shouted, "Goodbye, Mom!"
Then closed the door
and flipped the switch
And counted...

5

He closed his eyes...

and held on tight.

The engines went...

BoOm

Then there he was, in deep blue space...

...heading for the moon.

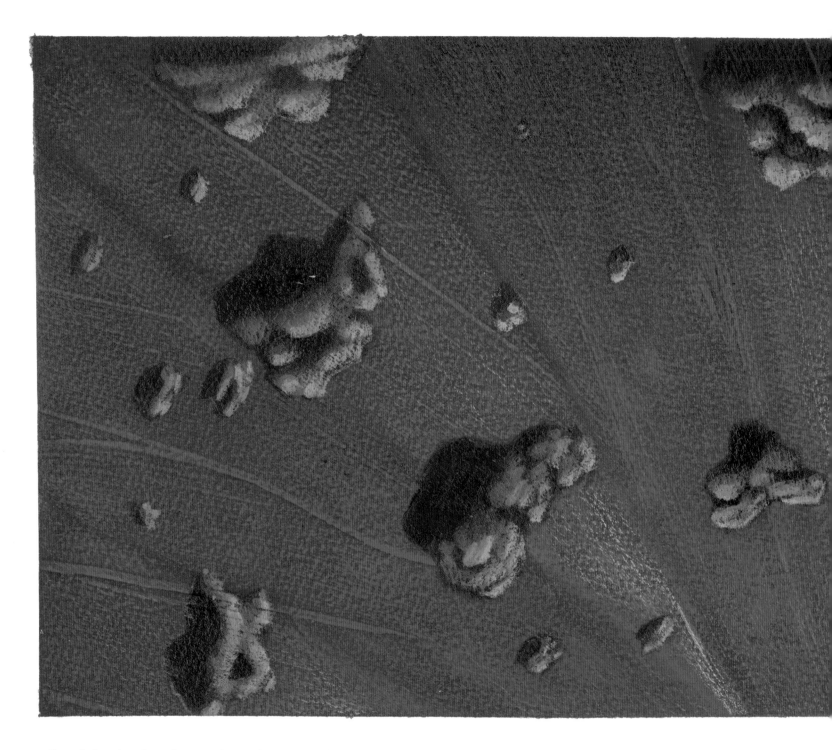

Suddenly he heard a bang. "The rocket's lost all power!"
He looked outside and thought, "Oh no! I'm in a meteor shower!"

A rock had hit his ship real hard and left a nasty crack.
Edward told his teddy bear, "We might not make it back!"

Then Edward heard another noise. A giant UFO!

But when he looked, an alien waved and offered him a tow.

They took him for some quick repairs and fixed his broken ship

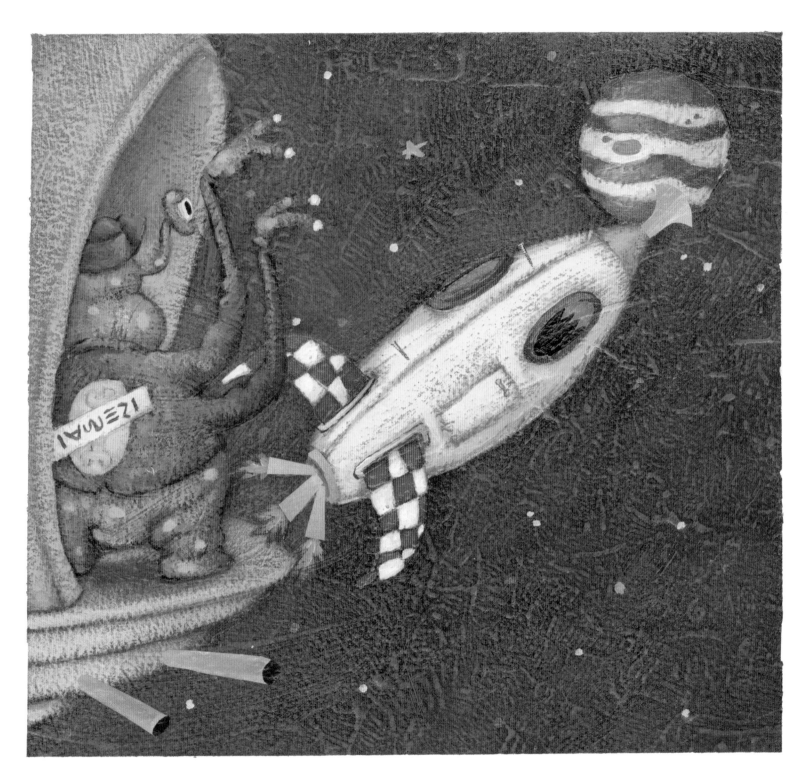

Then off he went to Jupiter, continuing his trip.

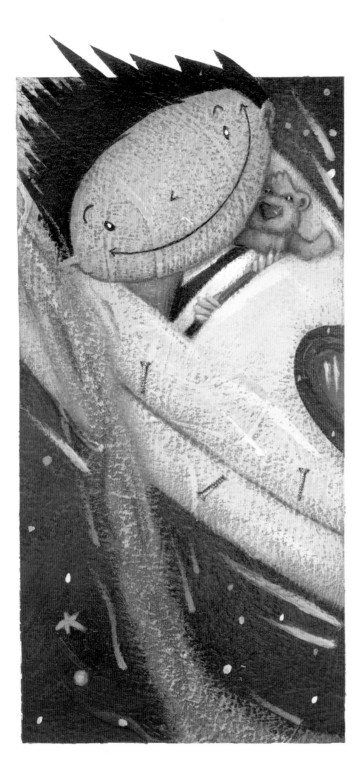

He drove around the Universe,
And chased an asteroid.

Saturn, Neptune, Uranus
Were planets he enjoyed.

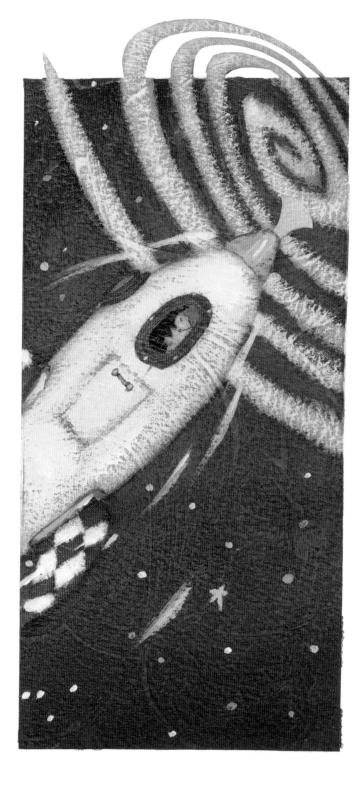

He waved at passing astronauts,
And steered past satellites.

He headed for the Milky Way
To look at all the sights.

18

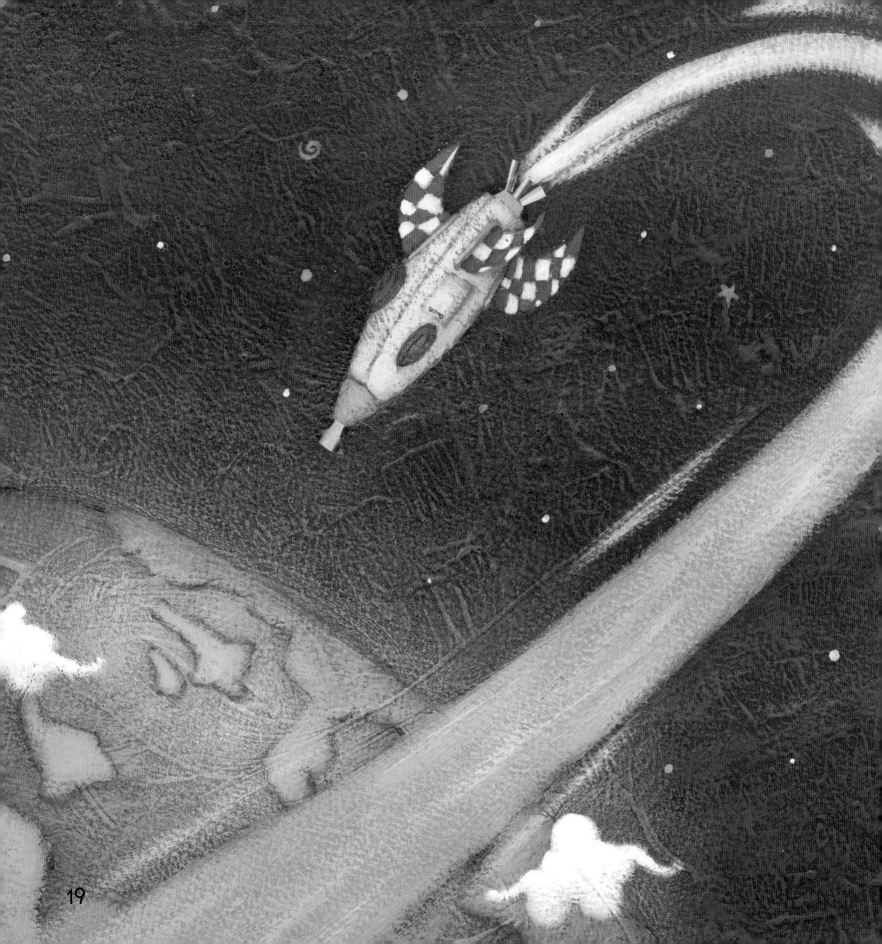

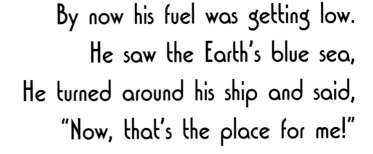

By now his fuel was getting low.
He saw the Earth's blue sea,
He turned around his ship and said,
"Now, that's the place for me!"

So he and Teddy dropped to Earth,
Strapped tight into their seats.
He pulled a cord that launched a chute
He'd made from Mommy's sheets.

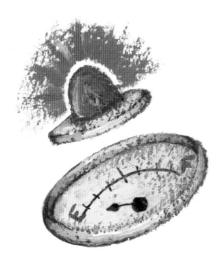

He floated down through fluffy clouds and rode in on the breeze.
Then finally he saw his house and landed in the trees.

He ran into his mother's arms and said, "I've touched the sky!

I've made a billion stars my friends...

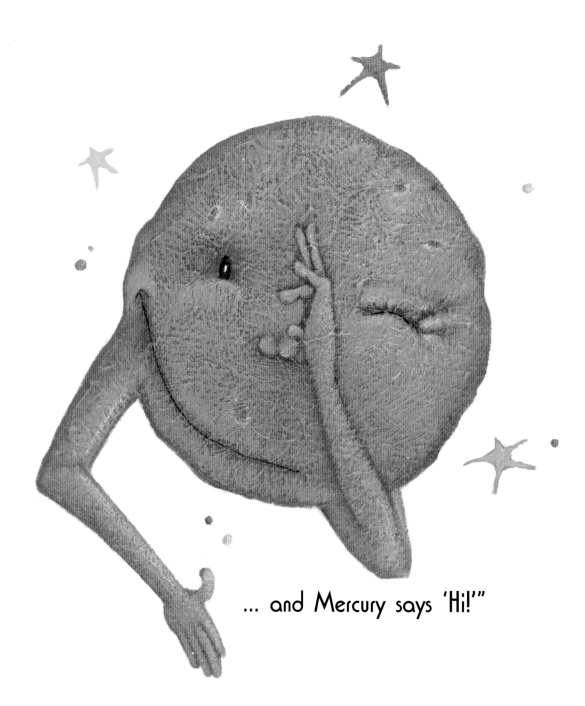

... and Mercury says 'Hi!'"